HAS ANYONE HERE SEEN LARRY?

Deirdre Purcell

LARGE
PRINT

First published in 2002 by
New Island
This Large Print edition published
2010 by BBC Audiobooks by
arrangement with
New Island

ISBN 978 1 405 62299 8

British Library Cataloguing in Publication Data available

Printed and bound in Great Britain by
CPI Antony Rowe, Chippenham and Eastbourne

For Maureen

1: What's in a Name?

It's not my real name, you know. Larry Murphy sounds to me like a builder with his trousers at half-mast. No, my real name is Larissa, a much classier name, I think you would agree. Mother gave me the name because my father was a Russian sailor.

This, of course, was a scandal, especially in those times. Poor Mother, who was only 20 years old, was quickly married off to my stepfather, who was much older than she. He ran a small dairy in Cork Street, near where she and her own family lived. He and Mother never had children of their own. Since Mother was an only child, I had no cousins either. So I was sort of an orphan in my own home as I was growing up.

A charity case, too, as the dairy

man reminded me almost every day of my life. Although I suppose I shouldn't judge him too harshly. Those times were different.

In those days of big families, to be an only child was to be a freak. In my case even more so because I was born on the wrong side of the blankets. (Since we all lived in each other's pockets there were no secrets in Long Lane.)

Anyway, to get back to how I got my name. Everyone in the Liberties in those days had a nickname, so I suppose I couldn't escape. And so 'Larry' I became forever. Sometimes, I think that naming me Larissa in a world of Nellies and Joans was the last brave thing Mother could do before she settled down to a hard life of work.

Secretly, I love the idea that I am half-Russian and with such a romantic name. No one talks of it now and I no longer mention it. Only in my own mind.

All right, I know that everyone sees only Poor Old Larry, the 87-year-old pain in the corner of the room. Poor Old Larry who can't even get up the stairs any more and who has to have a commode beside the bed at night.

Inside, however, Larissa is still 17 and golden. Instead of wearing cardigans day and night, even in bed, she always wears soft silks and satins. And while Poor Old Larry has to walk slowly with the aid of a stick, golden Larissa skips and hops down the road outside. She tosses her hair so that people always turn their heads to admire her fine skin, her slim, tall body.

Yes, Larissa is a princess who deserves life's little luxuries.

I would be happy enough with the ordinary stuff, never mind luxuries, if I could have it. Here I am in the closing years of my life and I have no say at all in anything I do. Even what I eat! Since the arthritis got bad and 'they' decided I could no longer mind myself, Martha had to come to live with myself and Mary. You see Mary works, and I need someone to be around during the day. Money-wise it was no hardship for her to move here because she had been in a rented flat.

I don't find it easy. She and I stagger along from day to day with one row following another. It wears me out, to tell you the truth. It is a terrible thing to lose your independence.

You know, it is still a surprise to me how two such different girls as Martha and Mary came out of the same womb. (They are hardly girls any more, of course, they are both in their fifties now.) But isn't it amusing that my late husband Josie and I called them Martha and Mary just because we liked the names, and yet they have become so like the Martha and Mary in the Bible. It is almost as if somehow we knew in advance what they would be like.

No wonder the Bible Martha complained. There she was, the poor thing, slaving in the kitchen to make the place nice and to make food for Jesus when He visited. Mary, on the other hand, didn't lift a finger to help, just sat at His feet rubbing oil into them and listening to His stories.

And what did Martha get for her pains? A lecture from their guest that her sister had chosen the 'better part'.

Not that I read the Bible. As a matter of fact, I don't even go to Mass any more. No need. I've heard enough Masses and priests during my long lifetime to see me safely into heaven. If there is a heaven at all.

So do people grow into their names?

2: Martha Speaks

Here is an example of what goes on in this house. Here is *my* day-to-day life. I get up at ten minutes past six. Before I bring Mammy her cup of tea—her first cup of tea, I might add—I have the washing in the machine and last night's load out on the line, rain or shine. (I have a special raincoat for going out to the line.) 'Good morning, Mammy,' I say as cheerfully as I can when I push open her door. I put the tea on her little table. Of course all I get in return is a grunt.

I try to ignore this and go back downstairs where I put on the porridge for the three of us. I slice up the bread for toast and lay the table. It is a quarter to seven by this time. When the porridge starts to simmer, I tramp back up the fifteen steps with Mary's cup of tea. I don't bother to bid her good morning. There is no point. She is in cloud cuckoo land, that one. All the time. I could be Godzilla coming in with a hatchet for all she knows or cares.

I go back into Mammy's room and find she hasn't even *touched* the tea. So I have to make her sit up. 'Drink that now, Mammy,' I say each day, as though for the first time. 'It will wake you up. And I'll be back in a minute or two to help you into your dressing-gown. The porridge is on.' She'll squeak something about it being too cold to drink. But I tell her it's her own fault. I try to be gentle about it—and of course I take it back down the stairs to put a hot drop into it.

When I have her sitting up and drinking, it's downstairs again. Then upstairs to check on the two of them. Then downstairs. I'm like a yo-yo. Same thing every day. Sometimes I think I should just record everything on a tape recorder. Then all I would

7

have to do is to switch it on every morning.

It is a quarter past seven before we are all sitting at the table. I am already wrecked.

The whole day is still ahead of me, of course. Dishes, shopping, cleaning, laundry, cooking. Driving Mammy to get her pension or to have her hair done—the bit of hair she has left. All right, it is her car and I have the use of it. But she can't drive it any more, can she?

She has the travel pass, of course, but would you let an 87-year-old out on her own to cross the city on a bus? So once a week I have to drive her to visit her pal who is so out of it she can't talk any more. All she can do now is to smile.

The visits to that nursing home are torture to me. I know I should have more patience with her, with the two of them indeed. After all, it is not poor old Marian's fault that she's as feeble as she is, but I can't help it. It is torture for me sitting there, watching Mammy whispering into her ear as if we have all the time in the world. All I can think about is that back home the washing is getting rained on.

Daddy slaved all his life and paid his insurance stamps, and for what? Because Mammy is not living alone, she is not entitled to any home help. So I'm not only *her* body slave, I'm a body slave to the State.

I asked Mary once if she could do something about getting Mammy some rights. After all, what is the use of being in the civil service if you don't have even a little bit of pull. But it was no use. She said it was a different department—well I knew that much—and she had no contacts at all.

My bet is she didn't even try.

So the result of it is that all day long, every day, I have to put up with Mammy's long face and her constant sighing. Her telling me that I'm putting the groceries on the wrong shelf in the fridge. Her asking me over and over again what time it is. She can't read the dial of her watch any more.

That's the worst part. Because I know why she keeps wanting to know about the time. She wants to know when her precious Mary will be home.

3: Bananas and Other Fool Food

I'm the last of my own family. And my darling husband, Josie, died many years ago. I sometimes forget his anniversary until Martha reminds me.

The really awful thing is that I have to look at my snap albums sometimes so I can remember his face.

To be fair, life in this house is probably as hard on the girls as it is on me. Especially on Martha. She's the eldest of the six children Josie and I had. As I'm sure she has told you by now, at *length*, she does everything. All the cooking, cleaning, washing, shopping and driving. She is always busy, always organising, always rushing here and there. Despite not working 'outside the home', as they say these days, she never has time to bless herself.

Sometimes I think she trained somewhere in some secret boot camp. She certainly runs this house as though she is an army officer. Her kitchen floor is so clean it squeaks and the carpet in the hall always smells of Shake 'N' Vac. (She likes the vanilla kind.)

I am not saying that she is a bad person. Or that she is mean to me. At least not on purpose! Because there is so little I can do for myself. My arms are as stiff as old windscreen wipers so I do value all she does for me, I do really. There are even times when I feel sorry for her.

But what can I do about it?

She is so bossy and pushy, she is hard to love. I have to admit that right up front. Yes, she is my own flesh and blood, but that's the way it is.

Naturally, I try to keep my lips zipped. God knows, but who could blame me if now and then I come out with what I really feel? I might be 87 but I'm still a real person.

And although she would never admit it, she does make things harder on herself than she has to. I think she enjoys being a martyr.

For instance, I wish she would not insist on driving me to visit my friend, Marian. All the rest of them are gone now and she and I are the last of the gang. She's a sad case, thin as a whip, and so weak she doesn't get out of bed any more. Although I find it hard to see her like this, if I didn't keep up the visits I feel I might as well give up the ghost myself.

Isn't it funny with friends? You always feel you have to explain yourself to your family, but never to your friends.

I could get a taxi to go to the nursing home. It is not that far, only a couple of miles, so it would not be all that expensive. After all, I do have a little bit of money from my pension. But Martha won't hear of wasting money on those rascal drivers. They would see me coming, she says. Old ladies are fair game to them, she says.

To tell you the truth, she ruins the visit for me. By the time we get there my nerves are already in shreds because she has a hissy fit if traffic lights don't turn quickly enough. And then, while my pal and I are talking together, she stays in the room. She pretends not to listen but jangles her car keys to let me know that time is short.

And don't get me started on her cooking. Sometimes I feel my throat will burst if I have to eat one more plateful of mashed up vegetables 'because they're good for you'. The teeth aren't great, of course—but really! Surely in this day and age there should be some solution so we don't have to eat like babies? I do try to get the stuff down but Martha gets in a snit if I make a face. I can't show even for one second that I am less than thrilled when she plonks this gooey, grey-looking mess in front of me each dinner-time. If I so much as sigh, she snatches the food away and throws it in the bin. She shoves a banana under my nose. 'There—eat that!' she says, as though I'm a monkey.

4: Bella! Bella!

I love Italy, as I'm sure my mother has already told you. I have no idea what she has been saying in general, but I am sure that at least she has told you that.

It is what we talk about in the evenings when I come home from work. I tell her about the large hot spaces around the Vatican. The bright, wide Spanish steps. The lovely wall paintings by Fra Angelico.

I am so lucky to have been there. I am so lucky to be going there again two weeks from now, this time to Verona. We have been booked in to see an opera, *Aida*. That's the one with the elephants and the big parade. I can't wait. I believe it is one of those events you will never forget for the rest of your life.

Mammy will miss me, I know that.

But it is only for two weeks and I have to get away from here now and then, I just have to.

I am going with a group of singles. It's how I always travel. 'Travel hopefully', isn't that what they say? Well, I've travelled hopefully for nearly thirty years at this stage and so far I haven't arrived! It's nearly all women on these singles' trips. I've come to terms with this. You see, from day one, all of them were better looking than me.

Although Italy is great in that regard. Men have whistled at me, you know. Even as lately as about five years ago when I would have thought I was long past it. In Italy, a woman, no matter how plain or fat, is made to feel like a woman. I always come home in a much better mood than when I left here. I usually feel quite good about myself, in fact. If I had any get-up-and-go I'd go to live in Italy for good.

Well, maybe not. Not with Mammy

to look after.

Most of the time, I don't really mind having Martha here with Mammy and myself. I'm out most of the day anyway.

But Martha feels put-upon all the time. We have fights. We fight about really small things. For instance, I like strawberry yoghurt and I keep it in the door of the fridge. But Martha wants to keep the door of the fridge free for bottles and jars and cartons of milk. Because she is here all the time, she always gets her own way.

But since I bring in most of the money, shouldn't I have some say over the arrangements in the fridge? Her point of view is that since, according to her, I don't lift a finger around the house, and since she is the unpaid maid, I have no right to tell her how to stock 'her' fridge in 'her' kitchen.

I try to keep these fights quiet so they won't upset Mammy, but I'm sure she knows about them anyway.

Some of the fights are silent. Just looks and expressions. I have to walk on eggs every tea-time.

What is the big deal about giving me my tea when I come home in the evening?

I don't want her to do my washing either, but she insists, even after she turned all my knickers pink!

And I have never asked her to bring me up that bloody cup of tea in the morning—not once!

That's what she throws up at me whenever there's a row: 'And every morning, I have to go up and down those stairs like a yo-yo bringing you and Mammy cups of tea . . .'

To tell you the truth I would far prefer it if she didn't. I tried to tell her as much once or twice but she took it personally. As though I was complaining about the quality of the tea.

I think if it wasn't for knowing that the holidays are coming up every year I would not be able to put up with the kind of stuff that goes on in this house.

Mammy and I actually look forward to the evenings when Martha goes out to visit her friend, Father Jimmy.

Don't you think that's a little bit odd? After all, he is a priest. But she spends hours getting ready and after she is gone we have to open the windows to get rid of the wash of talcum powder that's left in her wake. He gives her holy pictures with 'God Bless You, Martha' written on the back of them. She gives him presents. Grapes, buns from the local bakery, stuff like that.

Stop the lights! It's all a bit iffy, if you ask me. It's none of my business, of course. And I shouldn't complain because when she's out, we can watch *Coronation Street* without hearing her banging pots and pans about in the kitchen as if they are our heads.

I know she's my sister and I suppose at some level I do love her, but she is driving me crazy. Roll on Italy. *Bella! Bella!*

5: Six Tiny Teeth

No, cooking was never Martha's strong point. She makes my morning porridge as best she can, God help her, but it's always lumpy. I try not to point this out but sometimes I can't help it. That puts her in yet another huff for the rest of the day.

And then there are my clothes. She washes and scrubs the good out of everything and totally ignores the fact that I don't mind a few stains. A little bit of dirt never hurt anyone. I actually like the smells buried in my cardigans and blouses. The memories of old perfumes.

I certainly prefer those smells to the bleachy, artificial smells of washing powder.

But I might as well be talking to the wall. It is as though she is set on washing away every little bit of my real self, my Larissa self.

Yes, it's hard. But at rock bottom I know it is better to live here, even under Martha's thumb, than to have to sit around like a stick in some nursing home with a whole pile of other sticks.

Right now, it is almost five o'clock on a rainy June afternoon and here I am, sorting again. I'm in 'my' room, which is actually the dining-room of the house. Martha bought me this chair, kind of like a hospital chair, with a hard seat and a straight back. She also got me this footstool in some charity shop.

She's in the kitchen, frying onions. I hate the smell of onions and what I want to do is to open the window and let in the smells of the wet garden. But she doesn't want to get flies all over the house. Even if I could find the energy to lift these old bones out of this chair, it's not worth the row.

I do spend a lot of my time each day sorting and re-sorting the bits and pieces I keep in a set of hat boxes. Old letters and newspaper cuttings so old that I cannot remember why I cut them out in the first place. Snaps of myself and Josie. Postcards. All the examination results and school reports.

I have a special box for my dearest things. A pearly shell Josie and I found on a beach during our honeymoon in County Cork. A strand of green glass beads he gave me on our wedding day. The little silver bell that decorated the top of our cardboard cake. These were the war years and there was no sugar, so everyone had pretend cakes. We were wed at six o'clock in the morning. You had to get married to suit the train timetables. In those days everyone stayed in Ireland for their honeymoon. There was no going off to Italy or Spain.

A miraculous medal that Mary brought home to me from Rome, blessed by Pope John the Twenty-Third. Six tiny teeth, the first lost by each of the children. A dance programme from the dress dance at the Gresham Hotel where I first met Josie. He was with another girl that night but came around to my work the next day in the Monument Creamery.

A plait of my own hair, wrapped in blue tissue paper. I was so proud of my hair when I was young. When I finally allowed it to be cut, I made sure the hairdresser plaited it first so I'd be able to keep it to show it to my grandchildren.

I have 11 grandchildren from my four in America. Ruth, Rebecca, John and James. But the 11 of them are all living their own lives and beginning to produce children of their own. So I now have three great-grandchildren as well. Those kids are modern Yankees, living quick, sure lives. I get snaps regularly, of little blonde boys and girls in front of their barbecues and shiny motor-homes. None of them would be interested, probably, in a faded plait wrapped in blue tissue. Even if they were here.

I keep the birth certificates of my own six in a special little file. Imagine! Once upon a time I raised six children!

6: Father Jimmy

Precious Mary, with her Italian and her soft hands that never saw a bit of Flash or a drop of Domestos. Who does she think cleans the toilets around here? The toilet fairy?

If it comes to that, who do they both think I am? Their body slave?

Actually that *is* what I am, when you come to think of it. It's just not fair, is it?

Father Jimmy tells me that I shouldn't be giving out so much— that there'll be a special golden crown for me in heaven. Yeah, right. All I ask for is a bit of appreciation in this life.

I don't know what I'd do without Father Jimmy. He's my life saver. Some evenings I'm able to slip away from here for a few hours and we go to the pictures together, Father Jimmy and I. He's a holy man, of course. I wouldn't dream of thinking of him as anything but a priest. But he's good fun. I always look forward to our evenings out together. It's usually the pictures, or a lecture in the RDS, or a piano recital or something.

We just love the pictures, though. Father Jimmy knows a lot about them. He keeps up with all the latest ones. He's a friar so he doesn't have any money. I have to pay in for him but it is an honour. Why shouldn't I take it out of the housekeeping money? I tell you, the kids in McDonald's work half the hours I work and get paid for their effort. What do I get paid for all my work?

Going places with Father Jimmy from time to time keeps me from going mad. He has one of these big open faces with freckles and a great smile, with this gap between his front teeth. And when he says Mass, I just love the way he handles the altar vessels, so gently. Unlike other priests I could name who treat those precious things as if they've been bought in Hector Grey's. Father Jimmy has great hands, like a dancer's or an artist's. And although his hair is quite grey now, I'd say that when he was young he was a blondie. He has those whitish, stubby eyelashes and pale blue eyes.

I'm different when I'm with him. I'm able to relax. I even get to laugh a bit. I can think of myself as a real person. Even, dare I say it, as a woman. That's because he is so polite, holding the door open for me and so on. You probably wouldn't recognise me if you only know me as the drudge around this house because I go to a bit of trouble for him. I put on a little lipstick and powder.

Yes, he's a special person and I'm very lucky to have him as my friend.

But when I'm coming home on the bus, the nearer I get the more I imagine the front door of the house getting taller and wider. It opens up to swallow me like the jaws of a big trap. The more fun I've had, the worse looking the trap.

I don't know how it's going to work out tomorrow night. Tomorrow is Saturday and Father Jimmy is coming here to have tea with us. He's been here before of course, but only for a few minutes at a time, to say 'hello' to Mammy.

But the last time he was here didn't she up and invite him. And as I said, tomorrow's the night.

I don't know if I'm excited or fearful. I suppose deep down I'm afraid she and Mary will ruin it some way for me. How I don't know. But some way.

Sometimes I just feel like running away to Australia. Then they'd be sorry.

7: Here Comes The Monk

Tonight's the night. The salad sandwiches and fruit cake are already on the table, covered with damp tea-towels. Martha has bleached and starched the napkins until they are as white and stiff as shoe boxes. I'm sitting here, as washed and polished as her kitchen floor and under strict orders not to touch anything. 'My' room is no longer mine and I'm afraid to move in case I dirty the air.

Father Jimmy, as Martha calls him, is coming to tea. The place is in such a holy uproar you would think it was the Pope coming instead of just a humble monk. And to think I was the one who invited him! Me and my big mouth. I'll just have to grin and bear it, I suppose.

Mary could not stick it. She went out at about four o'clock. To get her hair done, she said. I think that was just an excuse. The last straw for her was when Martha hounded her up the stairs to change her pop socks because there was a ladder in the heel.

I sure hope she gets back before he arrives. Maybe she won't come home at all until he's safely gone. Dear God. That means I'll have to be on my own with the two of them.

What was I thinking when I invited him? As I told you, it just popped out of my mouth. I suppose in a way I was trying to please her.

The music she has on is getting on my nerves too because she has fixed it on 'repeat'. *Faith of Our Fathers*— the same thing over and over again. It was grand the first time, even the second time. I was always a big fan of Frank Patterson. But I've been listening to those dratted hymns now all afternoon and I'm sick of them.

Mind you, the next record, the one she's going to put on while we're having our tea, is also Frank Patterson. Frank singing duets with Count John McCormack. I suppose she thinks it's suitably clerical. It will certainly be a blessed relief.

She's out there now, rattling away, polishing the brasses for the third time this week. My eye.

The brasses don't need doing.

She's out there for one reason and one reason only. To watch for him.

Why couldn't Mary and myself be left alone to live together in peace. Although I have never said it out loud until now, you may have already guessed that secretly, I prefer Mary to Martha. She is the third in the family, after Martha and John.

'They' say that the third child is always the one to give trouble. Well, Mary is the living proof that sometimes 'they' are wrong. As a child, she was always the one with her nose stuck in a book. She has a job in the civil service, quite junior, I suppose, but good and steady, and with a pension to look forward to. She has no worldly ambition, really, except not to get hassled. I like that. She is the kind of quiet person who keeps her eyes and ears open and is always full of the wonders of the world. Smelling the daisies, I think they call it. It is restful to be around her.

She has a kind of special status here, the way the political prisoners used to have in the H Blocks up north. Since all I have is the few shillings from the widow's pension and since Martha brings in not a brass farthing, it is only right that Mary doesn't have to do any of the housework. After all, she has enough to do with her job. Brain work is as tiring as working with your hands, even more tiring perhaps. I would truly believe that because Mary is always exhausted when she comes home in the evening.

So after tea, while Martha washes up, Mary puts her feet up. She reads her books, or we watch something on television and eat chocolate or Fig Rolls. It's such a relief after all Martha's vegetables and things that are good for me! And so lovely and soft on my poor old gums! We have grand, slow discussions about what we're watching. Sometimes, as a special treat, she rubs my feet with her hand lotion. My corns are very bad these days.

Or I listen to her Italian verbs. Because she loves Italy so much, she is learning the Italian language. She bought me one of those really bright halogen lamps so I could read her text book and help her with her vocabulary. You see my eyes are nearly as bad as my feet. Hey folks, the big news is that there is nothing good about getting old!

I don't have any problem with her going on her holidays, she deserves it. But from my point of view, it's like a desert around here during those two weeks every year. The only good thing about it is looking forward to my present—a shell necklace, or a little box lined with mother-of-pearl, or a delicate fan. Always something really pretty. Mary has great taste.

I was surprised she never got married. Lucky for me, of course.

As for poor Martha—the girl is such a fuss pot, who'd have her?

It's unfair of me to say that. I sometimes think that since Martha works so hard and does all the practical things for me, it's very unfair that I prefer Mary. But there you are. It's a long time since I thought there was anything fair about this world of ours.

The rattling at the letter box has stopped and I can hear voices. The Great Man is here. And I think I hear Mary too. Thank God for small mercies . . .

8: Martha's Mad Tea Party

The monk comes in to the sitting room as does Mary. She is pink about the ears and smelling of hair spray. 'Hello!' says Father Jimmy cheerily to me. 'And how are we this afternoon? How is my absolute favourite little granny?'

I don't take offence. When you're my age, you get used to being talked down to. It's 'we' this and 'we' that. 'We' get to brush 'our' hair and 'we' get to lace up 'our' shoes every morning.

There's something about people talking in that way which makes you act like that. So I go all coy as I shake his hand, fine and plump and white. 'Hello!' I chirp back at him. 'I'm grand, thank you for asking.'

'Isn't this a great wee party?' He plops down on the sofa. It is quite a big plop. Father Jimmy is no light weight.

'It sure is.' I am smiling so widely my teeth might fall out. Which reminds me that I need more Fixodent. But I keep smiling. I am trying to be nice for Martha's sake, but God alone knows why. It's not as if this fella could be a son-in-law.

Mary sits down too: 'How are things down in the monastery, Father?'

'Oh, fine, fine. The usual—you know—all men together. Brother Mark does his best. You should see his collection of cookery books, but there is nothing like the woman's touch!' His eyes dart over to the table and I can see him undressing the food.

If this is what passes for fun conversation between the monk and Martha, she's welcome to it.

Martha catches me sniggering and glares. She hasn't sat down, of course. She is so jittery, poor girl, that she can't. Instead, as if she is reading Father Jimmy's thoughts, she starts whipping the covering off the food.

Now she's backing to the door: 'I'll just go and put the kettle on, Father, shall I?' And she's gone, speeding into the kitchen, leaving the three of us to continue our conversation as if we were at a garden party in Buckingham Palace.

I have to say that the tea, when Martha does bring it in, is lovely. Little fairy cakes and, as well as the salad sandwiches already on the table, a proper ham salad with dressing she made herself. She has rolled up the ham into hollow sausages and decorated them with cocktail sticks and tiny onions. Father Jimmy stands up from the sofa immediately—or rather, he rolls off it. We all sit down to eat.

Father Jimmy bows his head and says Grace. I'm too old for this, I think, but I bow my head anyway. I always feel uneasy now when God is brought in like this, in public, as if it is taken for granted that we are all of the same mind and heart. But how do they know if I am still a Catholic? I could be a secret Protestant, or a Hindu, for all they know. Nobody bothers asking these days, of course.

'They' say that old people should be saying their prayers. To tell you the truth, it is far from praying I spend my time. I doze or try to make up little stories in my head to take my mind off the pains and aches. Or I daydream a lot, usually about small things. I might think of the day all six of them went on strike and said they would not eat one more fish finger. Or the autumn day Josie took off work and, while they were all at school, swept me off on a mystery bus tour. We ended up in the Pine Forest where we sat on a wooden bench to eat our sandwiches. The smell of the trees . . .

Small things like that.

'Amen,' I say like a good little granny when Father Jimmy blesses himself at the end of the Grace. We start the tea.

The row blows up out of nowhere. One minute we are sitting, four points on the cross, the next, all hell has broken loose.

9: Crash! Bang! Wallop!

I don't know where to start. Mary and I are going out of our minds with worry. Here we are at Mammy's bedside in this hospital in Cork.

Yes, you heard right. The city of Cork.

There is nothing we can do except to sit here, listening to that awful bellows thing keeping Mammy alive.

But for how long? How long will they give us before they switch it off?

Will they do it just as soon as all the others have arrived from America and said their good-byes?

Oh my God, are we going to have to make this decision?

We have about 48 hours, that's when they'll all be here. Rebecca, who has to come from California, will be the last.

This is awful. We had no idea Mammy was capable of doing such a thing.

To vanish, just vanish. With just that measly note that we all misread—I wouldn't wish the last 24 hours on my worst enemy.

Thank God that she took her pension book with her so that when it happened we could at least be contacted.

Although what she thought she was doing with it, I don't know. I mean how long was it going to be before somebody noticed that a woman of almost 90 was wandering about by herself, with only a stick for company.

God, please keep her safe.

Please, please, Hail Mary Full of Grace, the Lord is with thee . . .

God, please, we're not ready. Please make her get better. Just for another little while. I promise I'll never say a cross word to her again. Ever in my whole life.

I'm sorry, Mammy. I'm sorry I shouted at you and made you upset about such stupid things as stains on a carpet. I'm sorry about the row.

And it was such a stupid row. It was just that I was so upset that she was having a go at Father Jimmy.

Dear God, please let her come back to us. Just for a while. Just so I can make it up to her. It was all my fault. I should never have made such a fuss.

Mammy . . . please, please wake up. Wake *up*, Mam. Why won't you wake up?

Listen, you old cow, you're doing this on purpose, aren't you? Just to punish me . . .

10: Just A Jaunt

In bed the night of the sad tea party, listening to the low murmur of my bedside radio, I went back over it all. If Father Jimmy and Martha fall out over this, I thought, she'll blame me and my life will not be worth living. If I was in the whole of my health, or just a bit younger, what I should probably do is lie low for a bit.

The more I thought about it, the more a break from my humdrum, boring old life sounded really great. As a matter of fact, a break from each other would do all three of us the world of good.

Killarney popped into my mind.

Josie and I had always planned to go there to see the lakes from the back of a jaunting car. We got as far as Glengarriff on our honeymoon, and we were so happy there, we never moved on. Even though

County Kerry was just at the end of the road.

I got so excited I sat up in the bed. Why not? I thought. I knew I wouldn't be able to manage a jaunting car, but I could find some way to see those lakes. It would give us all a break. I would take my travel pass and my money and I would go first thing tomorrow.

Then I had to plan how to do it. If I said anything to them in advance, they'd try to stop me. So I decided I wouldn't tell anyone, that I would just go, leaving a note so they wouldn't worry.

I couldn't sleep for excitement.

*　　　*　　　*

I'll never forget that knock on the door, never. Martha was hammering away at the telephone, ringing every hospital in Dublin. Who would have thought to start ringing hospitals in Cork?

46

I had to admire the way Martha immediately swung into action. She had even rung the nursing home where Mammy's friend, Marian, lives. When the knock came, she was running around the pubs in the Liberties. Mammy's travel pass was missing, and she does love that area of the city. And the publicans usually have their ear to the ground. She could have managed a bus, we thought, but we never, ever imagined she would have what it takes to actually leave Dublin.

As for me, I was feeling totally helpless, as usual. It was so sad to see the little footstool Mammy always used and her magnifying glass on top of her slippers any old how. Mammy is very neat. She must have left in quite a hurry.

When I answered the door and saw the policeman and policewoman, I was so afraid of what news they brought that I couldn't speak to ask them in. They came in anyway.

There had been an accident, they said, in Killarney.

Martha and I looked at one another.

Killarney?

We told the police there must have been some mistake.

But of course there hadn't been . . .

11: Look, Ma! No Hands!

It is an amazing feeling to be hanging between life and death. You are literally floating, about six feet above yourself, looking down on your poor tired body and everything that's going on.

I must point out, though, that there are no lights or tunnels or anybody standing at the bottom of the bed smiling and holding their hands out to you.

I had always hoped that I would find my darling Josie again. Maybe that comes later.

But it is very interesting. All everyone down there sees is your body, quiet as a corpse. But you can hear what they are saying. Not only that but you can read their thoughts!

Poor Mary. Poor Martha.

I don't want to be causing such pain to my two daughters—or to the others either, when they come. But the strange thing is that although in life I would have felt as upset for them as they are for themselves, at present I feel totally calm, as if their pain has nothing at all to do with me.

It's a lovely feeling actually. I would recommend it.

As for my body down there, I look like a Dalek in my opinion, with all those tubes and cables. But actually, I feel quite comfortable. I don't have to do anything at all, or be anything other than what I am. All I have to do is to live right in this present moment. To be.

I feel free. Freer than I have been since I was a girl.

Poor Martha. All that grief.

Poor Mary. She'll deal with it better, I think. Less to regret.

I suppose the others are all packing now and getting ready to board flights. I wonder what they're telling their kids. My grandchildren.

I never saw that coach coming until

it was too late. Honestly.

There has been some discussion that I stood there deliberately, waiting for it to hit me. Nobody actually says the bad word, but they're all half-thinking it. Suicide.

No. I promise that wasn't what happened. I just froze. I knew I hadn't the time to get out of its way so I didn't try.

It was so big. Huge. The last thing I remember is the size of it, rearing up over me like a ship coming on to a rowing boat. And the big round 'O' of the driver's mouth as he tried to pull the monster aside to avoid me.

I could even tell you what was written on a white card taped to the inside of the huge window: Coach 3.

My last waking thought was an absurd one. Where are Coach 1 and 2?

I am sorry now that I did what I did—or I would be if I could feel anything other than this lovely sense of easy peace.

It was selfish. I see that now.

And if I was feeling normal, I would feel guilty about that poor coach driver and all those poor shocked Americans. There was even a little child there, crying her eyes out.

But like everything else, I see my selfishness and my guilt in the distance, wrapped up in two tidy little balls. Everything is in tidy little balls at the moment, all the feelings and events and hurts. Even all the good things. My life all parcelled up and ready for the post. It's just me now, part of the air.

I feel I could fly out that window over there without it even being opened for me. Like Super-man.

And there is no pain.

12: A Load of Old Bones

Like I told you, the row at Martha's tea party blew up out of thin air.

We had been talking about all the usual things people talk about in Ireland these days. In my day it used to be the weather and de Valera. Now it is crime and the price of houses and asylum seekers.

So we were discussing these things when, in all innocence, I asked Father Jimmy what did he think of the St Thérèse-mobile. Honest to God, I promise I asked it only to keep the conversation going. But Martha fires up immediately. 'For God's sake, Mammy, don't start!'

Mary jumped in then: 'Leave her alone. She was only asking—

'She wasn't. She was trying to stir things up—

Father Jimmy was looking from one to the other of them. There was a bit of salad dressing dribbling down his chin but he didn't even notice. 'Please,' he said, 'Please. It is a perfectly ordinary question. I'll be glad to talk about it—

Martha was as mad as hell, of course, but there was nothing she could do.

'Now, Larry,' he turned to me, 'what is your own opinion on the St Thérèse-mobile?'

The St Thérèse-mobile, in case you have been living in outer space, is the car that carries the bones of The Little Flower—St Thérèse of Lisieux—all around Ireland. I am not quite sure exactly what bones are here, I haven't paid all that much attention, but I think it might be her arm. And maybe a shin. They came in from France on the ferry and were carried ashore by Irish soldiers.

Whichever bones are here, there are hundreds of thousands of people turning up to every crossroads, church and chapel all over the country to honour them. I even hear about it on AA Roadwatch on the radio, where they give drivers advance warning of where and when the relics are due to arrive.

Anyway, to get back to the row.

I didn't pay much attention to the way Martha was fuming, because of course I was used to it. She was up on her high horse about my question because she thinks I am anti-clerical and anti-church. Just because once or twice I happened to remark that I thought it was pretty weird to be hawking a load of old bones around the place. (I do too.)

For the sake of peace, though, I didn't say this to Father Jimmy. 'What do I think?' I said to him. 'I don't think about it much one way or the other, Father. I'm hardly going to get to see them in any case—

Martha immediately took this as a criticism of her care of me. 'That's not fair, Mammy. How dare you behave as though you are locked up here. I take you out in that car every week to see your friend, Marian— and to get your hair done any time you want. And what about every Friday to get your pension? I stand there like a poodle in that post office while you dawdle and mess about, chatting to people. I could be doing better things you know.'

As she carried on, I saw that the situation had got out of hand. Mary, for instance, was going bright scarlet. Father Jimmy had put down his knife and fork.

In fairness to poor Martha, the reason she was so uptight in the first place was because Father Jimmy was here and it would have taken very little to light her fuse. I also knew she was doubly upset because now he was seeing the worst side of her and yet she wasn't able to stop herself.

I couldn't shout her down. One of the things that is bad about old age is that your voice gets very weak. You don't have the breath, you see.

So the only way to stop her, to save her from herself, I suppose, was to keel over.

So I did. I closed my eyes and let my head fall forward onto the plate. (Of course I couldn't reach the plate. Too stiff.) My neck hurt like hell, but I hung there, grimly, trusting it would work.

It did. For a moment there was stunned silence. Then: 'You've killed her.' This was Mary, in a low, frightened voice.

So I gave a little whimper and opened my eyes.

There was a lot of thanking God and patting me on the back and giving me sips of water and asking me if I needed my heart patch or something to put under my tongue. After a few minutes, I did manage to persuade them that I was all right, but the row hung over us all like a bad smell.

Although we tried to recover, praising the fairy cakes and eating far too many of them, the evening just lay there like a dead duck.

I felt so sorry for Martha, she had gone to so much trouble, but what could I do?

13: 20/20 Vision

Another thing that's good about my present state is that I have 20/20 vision. Without my specs, I can clearly see everything in this room. Even in the farthest, darkest corner. For instance, over there behind that oxygen yoke, is a tiny spider's web, only about half-an-inch wide. I bet someone sure would get into trouble if I mentioned that!

The train journey to Killarney was a breeze. In fact it was delightful, giving the lie to what is said nowadays about our uncaring society. I waited until Martha—who was still in a post-tea-party huff—had left to go into town. Then, as soon as the front door slammed behind her, I telephoned for a taxi.

From the moment I stepped into that taxi, everyone was so helpful. I truly enjoyed myself. The taxi-driver carried my bag for me at Heuston station. The ticket checker even signalled to the train guard to come and help me into the carriage and—here comes the best bit—this lovely guard escorted me all the way to the front of the train. He didn't even seem to mind how slow I was, chatting away as we moved along. 'In here, Missus,' he said when we'd reached the top carriage. 'We're a bit crowded this morning, but don't say a word. I'll sort it out with everyone.'

First Class! Imagine! Me! Larry Murphy from Long Lane! They bring you your food to the table. Did you know that? And the seats are so comfortable, they even have arm rests. The last time I travelled by train I was sitting on a hard bench seat covered with this green-checked fabric that was so slippy and greasy I kept sliding off it.

Anyway, after a brilliant journey, we got to Killarney. There, too, the people could not have been more helpful.

I asked the platform guard if he could recommend a hotel nearby. 'It doesn't matter if it's expensive,' I said, 'it's only for one night.'

'No problem, Ma'am,' he said back, and before I knew it, he was carrying my bag and linking me down a little avenue to a *huge* hotel that seemed to be at the entrance to the station. But then, when we were nearly at the front door, he had to go back because someone was calling him to take a telephone call. 'Are you sure you'll be all right, Ma'am?' he asked me.

'I'll be fine,' I said. I meant it. I really felt great at that point.

So I took my bag from him and waved him off. Then I stood for a moment, getting my bearings.

A horse whinnied. It seemed to be quite close too, just beyond the railings. *Jaunting cars* . . .

So I left the bag down and set off for the entrance. I was almost there when this tourist bus turned in.

The mistake I made was to stop dead. I froze like a rabbit in the beam of a lamp. Even if I couldn't have got out of the way in time, at least if I'd tried, he might have missed me.

Next thing I knew, there was all this rushing around and people yelling and other people whispering and putting jackets under my head and this poor little American child crying and crying. I knew she was American because through her tears she kept calling on her 'Mommy' to 'wake up the old lady'.

Do you know what's really sad? Now I'll never get to drive in a jaunting car. Oh dear! Mary is reading that note again.

How could I have been so stupid as to write it in such a way that people could think it was a suicide note?

Dear Martha and Mary,
I am so sorry I have been such a bother to you both. Please don't be upset with me. I have wanted to do this for a long time.
All my love,
Mother

Actually, the note wasn't meant to be that short but the taxi-man started to ring the bell just as I was writing it. I was afraid that if I didn't get to the door quickly enough, he would leave. That happens a lot with us slow-coaches. So I just figured there was enough there to keep them going and scribbled the 'All my love, Mother' bit.

Oh no! Here's Father Jimmy! All the way down here. Who called him?

If I have to ask I must be one step closer to the pearly gates than I thought I was.

14: Decision Time

If praying was electricity, there is enough of it going on here to light up the country. Within minutes of his arrival, Father Jimmy and Martha hit the rosary beads and have been at it since, God love them. At least their Hail Marys and Holy Marys are drowning out the other sounds in this room, all the hissing and pinging and bleeping. I wish now they would open the window. The place is so air-tight it is a wonder any of them can breathe.

Are the others boarding their flights yet, I wonder? Or would they be in the air by now? I have completely lost track of time. The nurses come and go with their clipboards, carrying boxes of blood and little packets of needles. I don't know if it is day or night, to tell you the truth.

Mary is asleep, huddled in a corner over there with her head on her knees.

As for Martha, poor Martha. I can see she will not sleep properly for years, if I go now. She will blame herself. She will beat herself with all the harsh words she ever said to me. She will never be able to look a banana in the face again.

The really odd thing is that I know something they don't. I can make a decision. I can actually decide whether or not to leave them or to stay.

I think this is the very first time that I have had that power over my own life—and over theirs.

The temptation to float away is very strong. Josie is somewhere out there, and Mother. I don't give a toss about the dairy man. He was a cold, mean fish and although I hope that wherever he is, he is happy, hoping is not the same as caring.

So I could go. I have to go anyway,

sometime. And they're all prepared.

And it would be a pity to have the others waste their good money on flights, wouldn't it? I can just hear James giving out about such a criminal waste of money if he rushed here and found me sitting up in bed having a little egg. He's an accountant. From the time he could walk, he was saving money in a jam jar.

How disappointed would they be? On balance, I think Ruth and John would probably be glad to see me alive. But I have no idea what Rebecca would feel. She lives in California and I have lost touch with her. She does write, once a month, but it is hardly communication. I believe in my heart that she writes not because she wants to, but because she feels it is her duty. I have to make allowances, I suppose. Her brat of a husband ran off with another man and left her to raise her two little boys. It isn't easy being a single mother, even in the sunshine of California.

So I should give them a funeral to come back to, shouldn't I?

Mary would cope with my death, I think. She and I have a very good relationship and although she would be very sad, she would have few regrets. On the other hand, she is due to go to Italy soon. She might feel that she had to cancel. I would hate to be the cause of that.

What about Martha? She and I have a lot to resolve. Shouldn't I give us the chance? I don't want to be responsible for her living the rest of her life feeling guilty. And she has been good to me in her own odd way. If I'm to stay it will probably be for Martha . . .

I can see their feelings, the colours of them: Mary's are a soft salmon shade, Father Jimmy's are a deep purple. Martha's are a violent red. She desperately wants me to stay.

Sorry Josie.

15: Resurrection

My knees are sore, my head is sore. I can't even count the beads any more.

Mammy hasn't stirred for hours. I tried to squeeze her hand for a bit, to see if she would squeeze back, but there was nothing.

It's three o'clock in the morning. I'm alone with her at the moment. Father Jimmy and Mary have gone to the day room to make a cup of tea for themselves.

I'm afraid to leave here even for a second. It is said that they always wait until they're alone in order to go.

But I can't let her go, not yet.

I shouldn't have gone to the bank yesterday. If I had just come home straight from the shops I might have been in time to stop her going on the damn fool trip. What possessed her? Killarney? A jaunting car? The ambulance man who drove her to Cork told us that she came to for a minute or so as they were driving through Abbeyfeale and she whispered something about Daddy and a jaunting car.

'Mammy—can you hear me? I—I love you, Mammy. Don't go yet, please . . .'

*   *   *

Why do hospitals always have custard creams? I don't like custard creams.

Father Jimmy is quite nice really— Martha guards him so fiercely that I have never got to know him until now.

I don't know about this laying on of hands business, though. I think I would feel pretty silly. But I wouldn't like to offend him either.

I asked shouldn't all three of us do it, but he says Martha is too upset. That she would be better concentrating on the practical side of things.

I suppose it couldn't do any harm.

*   *   *

Well, Martha finally had to leave to go to the bathroom. They have persuaded her to make herself a cup of tea.

While she's in the day room, Father Jimmy has also asked her to check up on the flight arrival times on the Teletext. He says that the New York flight time might be up by now.

Now the other two are putting their hands on my body. Father Jimmy is at my head and Mary is rubbing my feet the way she always does. It's probably a very nice sensation. I don't feel it up here, of course.

Ah well—it's now or never.

16: Hello, Dolly!

It was worth coming back, even though freedom was only a step away, just to see Martha's joy when she entered the room.

I am not out of the woods, of course. I feel very weak and I know I will be in hospital for a while. But at least she and I will now have time to fix whatever was broken between us.

She nearly fainted when she saw my eyes open. It was Mary who told her how I came back: 'It was very quiet, Martha, real quiet. I wasn't even praying. Father Jimmy just had both hands on her head, one at the crown and one at the forehead. And I was just massaging gently.'

'The next thing, I could actually feel a movement in the sole of one of her feet and I looked up and her hand was moving too. And then her eyes opened, real slow . . .'

(I had to control it a little, not to give them too much of a fright.)

Martha fell on Father Jimmy. 'Thank God, thank you, Lord! It's a miracle—Father, you're a miracle worker, thank you, thank you!'

Right now she is still wringing his hand. 'I shouldn't have left. I should have been here—

'We were all playing our part, Martha.' Father Jimmy takes her hand and pats it. Probably to stop his own from being mangled. 'Don't fret,' he says, 'your Mammy is back with us, that's the main thing. Now I think we should get a nurse or a doctor, don't you? They should be told.'

He leaves the room to me and my two daughters. Although I want to hug them both, I am too feeble to raise my arms.

It is Martha who sees this. Careful not to disturb all the tubes and drips, she raises me gently and plumps up my pillows. And then she gives me a hug. In my living memory, this is the first time she has embraced me since her childhood.

I try to speak but if my voice was weak before it's a whisper now. They come close and I whisper at them to prepare the others. 'Tell them I'm sorry they've had a wasted trip. No funeral.'

'You could hear everything we were discussing?' Mary is crying—with joy I believe—but Martha is appalled now. Although I can no longer read her thoughts, I know my daughter. She is flipping back through the night, trying to remember what she has said, hoping against hope she has not given me any ammunition. Things are getting back to normal.

I smile at both of my beautiful daughters and it is no effort.

'I'm sorry for giving you both a fright,' I say. 'I'll never go away again.'